THE SCARY PLACES MAP BOOK

SEVEN TERRIFYING TOURS

Get ready for some of the most spine-tingling and hair-raising tours this side of Halloween! Say good-bye to safety and hello to danger when you join your ghoulish guides for a once-in-a-lifetime tour of seven scary places.

You will have a map and directions for each tour. Around the border of each map are letters and numbers to help you find your way and stay out of danger. A compass rose will show you the directions of north, south, east, and west. A key identifies local routes, special features, and distances. Stay with your guide — or you may never get back!

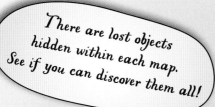

There are lost objects hidden within each map. See if you can discover them all!

B. G. HENNESSY

ILLUSTRATED BY ERWIN MADRID

CANDLEWICK PRESS

Main topsail

Mizzen sail

Foresail

Mizzenmast

Mainsail

Foremast

Captain's cabin

Mainmast

Officers' quarters

Anchor

Rudder

Gun deck

Ballast and stores

Bunks

THE GHOSTLY GALLEON

THE GHOSTLY GALLEON CRUISE OF THE SEVEN SEAS

Captain Davy Jones has charted a special cruise aboard his favorite ship, the *Ghostly Galleon*. From sea monsters to pirate islands, the cap'n and his sea dogs will make sure you don't miss a single bloodcurdling sight. See if you can find Scurvy Boy. He jumped ship on the last voyage and hasn't been seen since. The motto of this crew is "We'll put a shiver in your timbers!" So pack your spyglass, batten down the hatches, and get ready to set sail with the evening tide at lucky Pier 13 in Haunted Harbor, if you dare!

DANGER!

✦ **BERMUDA TRIANGLE**
The final resting place for many a sailor. This area of the ocean should only be crossed with a master navigator, or you may never return!

✦ **ALBATROSS**
If you spot an albatross, watch out! They are BAD LUCK!

✦ **KRAKEN**
A gigantic, octopus-like sea monster, found most often in northern waters.

THE *GHOSTLY GALLEON* CRUISE OF THE SEVEN SEAS

DIRECTIONS

- Board the *Ghostly Galleon* at lucky Pier 13 in Haunted Harbor (I4), and set sail with the tide.

- Head west along the Barbary Coast (H4, G4) for 300 mermaid leagues.

- Stop for grog in Tripoli (G4). Head west for 300 mermaid leagues through the Strait of Gibraltar (F4). Watch out for rogue waves!

- Sail northeast along the coast for 300 mermaid leagues. At London Town (F2), head north for 100 mermaid leagues.

- Sail west for 350 mermaid leagues across the mighty Atlantic. Keep a lookout in the crow's nest for icebergs and the Kraken.

- Sail southwest for 500 mermaid leagues. Avoid the Bermuda Triangle! Many a ship has been wrecked on its reefs.

- Land at Tortuga (B5), the captain's island home. Stop by his mother's house for tea.

- Sail southeast 150 mermaid leagues to the lovely Spanish Main (C5). Don't get becalmed in the doldrums!

- Then look shipshape, me hearties, and sail northeast 650 mermaid leagues back to London Town.

It takes a sharp sailor's eye to spot Scurvy Boy. Did you find him?

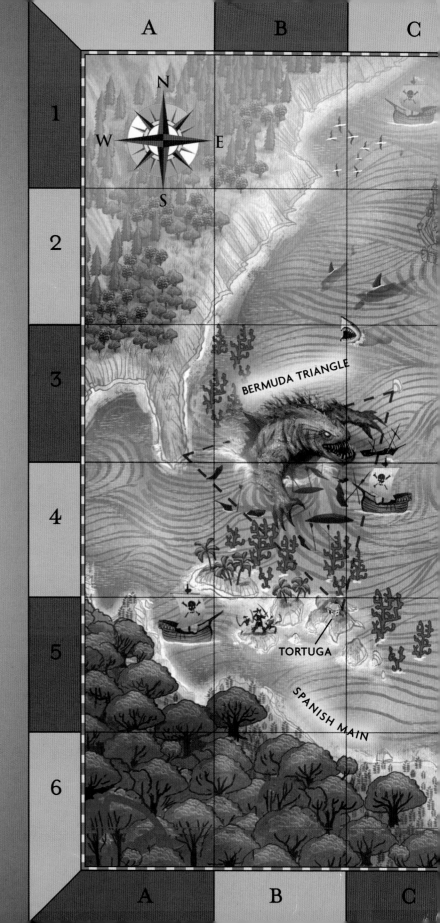

THE MINOTAUR'S LABYRINTH

LAND of MYTHICAL MONSTERS

Who better to lead a tour through the birthplace of the foulest, ugliest, and fiercest monsters of all time than Hercules, a legend himself. This tour is for experts only. Pack your best hiking shoes and sunscreen. Mighty Hercules will meet you at Athena's Temple. You will trek through snowcapped mountains, sail to the sunny island of Crete, and hike back to the dark door to the Underworld. Test your skills and see if you can make it through the Minotaur's famous labyrinth. Four of Zeus's buckets of thunderbolts are hidden along the way. See if you can find them.

DANGER!

- **HERA'S SECRET GARDEN**
  Don't touch the golden apples!

- **SIRENS**
  Bring earplugs to avoid hearing the Sirens' Song, or you won't return.

- **GORGONS**
  Never look directly at the snaky-headed Gorgon! You'll be petrified! *Really*.

- **HYDRA**
  A frightful creature with many heads. Chop one off and two grow back.

LAND of MYTHICAL MONSTERS

DIRECTIONS

✦ Begin the tour at Athena's Temple (E3). Look for the peak of Mount Olympus to the west (G4, H4).

✦ Follow the footpath from Athena's temple southwest for 3 Hercules strides to Hera's Secret Garden (J3).

✦ Then travel east 2 Hercules strides for a stop at the Stables of King Augeas, site of Hercules's big cleanup (G2). Then head southeast 1½ Hercules strides to Nemea (E1). Watch for the famous lion.

✦ To the northeast is Mount Erymanthos (D2). This is off our tour because of the return of the wild boar.

✦ Follow the footpath 2 Hercules strides east through the Swamps of Lerna and to the harbor. Beware of the lurking Hydra.

✦ Board the vessel *Helios* (C1) and sail 1 Hercules stride southeast to the island of Crete. There Hercules has arranged a VIP tour of the Minotaur's labyrinth.

✦ Sail back to the mainland, then follow the river upstream 2 Hercules strides to where it branches (B4). Head east ½ Hercules stride to Stymphalian Lake (B4). Stay away from the birds!

✦ Head north on the rocky path 2½ Hercules strides to the door to the Underworld. DO NOT ENTER.

✦ Return to the end of the rocky path and find the mountain path. Travel southwest 3 Hercules Strides for a lovely sunset view from Apollo's Temple at Delphi (E4).

Remember to look for the four buckets of Zeus's thunderbolts. They might come in handy on this journey.

Here lies the body of Margaret Bent She kicked up her heels and away she went.

JEDEDIAH GOODWIN AUCTIONEER BORN 1828 GOING! GOING!! GONE!!! 1876

It was a cough that carried him off

It was a coffin they carried him off in

Stranger tread this ground with gravity. DENTIST BROWN is filling his last cavity

TOMBSTONE'S BONE ORCHARD

ROUNDUP OF THE WESTERN TERROR-TORIES

Pull on your cowboy boots, grab your cowboy hat, and hop on the last stage to Tombstone. Gruesome Gus will meet you at the depot. He ain't pretty, but no one knows more about the Western Terror-tories. Saddle up and ride along Horse Thief Canyon to the Bloody Basin Road, then down, down, down to Phantom Ranch. Gus will make sure you see all the scariest places and hear all the chilling tales of the Wild West. You won't miss a thing—as long as you keep your eyes open. Keep a lookout for Mable, Gus's mule, but don't rile her—her pack is full of dynamite!

DANGER!

✦ **ABANDONED MINES**
Keep out! There are miles of underground tunnels— if you enter, you may never return!

✦ **QUICKSAND**
Look out for sandy patches—they might be quicksand.

✦ **RATTLESNAKES**
Their bite is worse than their rattle.

✦ **SCORPIONS**
Shake out your gear to make sure these stinging creatures aren't trying to hitch a ride.

ROUNDUP OF THE WESTERN TERROR-TORIES

DIRECTIONS

✦ Hop off the stagecoach in Tombstone (J1). Gruesome Gus will meet you at the depot. Before you head out, Gus will take you on a tour of the Bone Orchard (I1).

✦ Time to saddle up and head south 2½ bronco miles. Keep an eye out for bandits in Horse Thief Canyon (I2–3).

✦ At the end of the canyon, head northwest for 4 bronco miles along Bloody Basin Road, crossing Dead Man's Wash and heading toward Tabletop Mesa (F1–G1).

✦ Continue west 6 bronco miles. After Ghost Town (B2), head southwest 1 bronco mile to Vulture Peak (B2).

✦ Keep an eye open for the head of Tumbleweed Trail—it's the only way down into the canyon. The trail is treacherous; be careful your mule doesn't get spooked.

✦ When you finally reach the canyon floor, head east to the river—your mule deserves a good long drink. Follow the river 1 bronco mile southeast to Phantom Ranch (C6), where dinner will be waiting for you.

Did you find any sign of Mabel, Gus's mule?

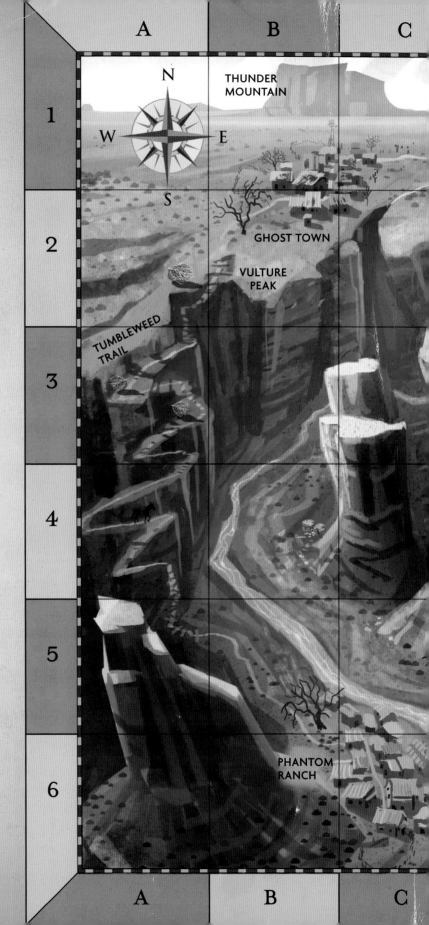

Tess's
Hexes

Crystals
& Curses
Bootique

BROOMINGDALES

Toil &
Trouble
Cauldron
Café

Spell
★ mart

SISTERHOOD
OF WITCHES
DAY SPA

Brotherhood
of Wizards
'n' Warlocks
Bookstore

WITCHFIELD VILLAGE

TOUR OF THE WICKED WOODS AND WITCHFIELD VILLAGE

You will want to be wide awake for this tour — who knows what, or who, might be lurking behind the next tree in the Wicked Woods. As soon as the moon rises, grab a broomstick and meet at the Gingerbread Cottage. The Wicked Witch will be leading this trip, and she doesn't like to be kept waiting. Included in the tour is a fortune-telling session and a special tasting of witches' brew at the Toil & Trouble Cauldron Café in Witchfield Village, the favorite vacation spot for wizards and witches. Who knows? You might be lucky and spot one of the celebrity sorcerers. There is a golden broomstick lost somewhere along your route — see if you can find it.

DANGER!

✦ **POISON APPLE ORCHARD**
These apples will *not* keep the doctor away!

✦ **TROLLS**
They don't take kindly to being disturbed. Best to steer clear.

✦ **SNOW QUEEN'S ICE CASTLE**
Exquisitely beautiful, but COLD!

Tour of the Wicked Woods and Witchfield Village

DIRECTIONS

✦ From Gingerbread Cottage (I6) take the Breadcrumb Trail northwest 10 broomsticks along the northern border of the Poison Apple Orchard.

✦ At Twin Trees, follow the Pebble Path west 7 broomsticks, then northwest 5 more broomsticks, to Toad Pond (F5). Continue on the sand path northeast to the Ogre's Manor (H4). From there, head north 10 broomsticks to the shore of Broken Spell Lake (G3) at the foot of Giant Forest.

✦ Continue west on the sand path for 12 broomsticks, then southwest 15 broomsticks, to Wizard's Waterfall. If there is a rainbow, make a wish!

✦ Cross Troll Bridge and pick up the Rocky Road northwest for 10 broomsticks to the top of Haunted Hill (C2), for a spectacular view of the Snow Queen's Ice Castle (C1–D1)

✦ From Haunted Hill, take Rocky Road west. Pick up Halloween Highway (B2), and travel southwest 10 broomsticks to the first exit for a brief stop at the Magic Potion Botanical Gardens.

✦ Return to Halloween Highway and continue south and east 27 broomsticks until you reach the gates of Witchfield Village.

✦ Leave your broomstick at the gate. The Wicked Witch will take you to your fortune-telling and lunch at the Toil & Trouble Cauldron Café.

Did you find the Golden Broomstick? You'll need it to get home!

DR. FRANKENSTEIN'S
LABORATORY

Trip Through Transylvania

At night, Igor still works for Dr. Frankenstein, but during the day, he leads the best tour in all of Transylvania. Looking for zombies, ghouls, banshees, or ghosts? Igor will make sure you see them all—and they see YOU! Dress warmly for a special tour of Dracula's castle and a stop at Dr. Frankenstein's laboratory. Meet at the train station in Haunted Hallows. Igor should be easy to spot: he'll be driving the Bloodmobile. Dracula's coffin is hidden somewhere in Transylvania. Try to find it along the way.

DANGER!

✦ **VAMPIRES**
Vampires are strong, quick, and dangerous.
Travel Tip: Keep some garlic and a lit torch nearby to keep them at a safe distance.

✦ **WEREWOLF WOODS**
The gem of the Transylvania Forest and home to a large pack of werewolves.

✦ **ZOMBIE LAKE**
A great place for a photograph, but looks can be deceiving: absolutely NO SWIMMING allowed here!

Trip Through Transylvania

DIRECTIONS

✦ Begin at the train station in Gremlintown (G6). Take the Banshee Express and get off at the Haunted Hallows stop (C4).

✦ Igor will be waiting in the Bloodmobile. Drive southwest 2 zombie miles to Dr. Frankenstein's lab.

✦ After the tour, take the Ghost Trail north for 3 zombie miles to the Ghostly Graveyard (B3). From here, you will have a lovely view of Halloween Hill (A2).

✦ Travel 2 zombie miles east on the Ghost Trail, passing through Skeleton Swamp. Pick up Bones Lane and follow Dracula Drive up to Dracula's castle for the guided tour.

✦ After the tour, return down Dracula Drive to Bones Lane. Follow it east for 6 zombie miles to the Bat Caves (H2) on Shadow Mountain.

✦ At the base of the Bat Caves, take the bridge over Devil River for a scenic drive through the famous Werewolf Woods southwest to Zombie Lake (H4).

✦ After a photo stop at Zombie Lake, take Dragon Drive west around the lake to the opposite shore, then turn south and travel 2 zombie miles back to Gremlintown.

Don't forget to look for Dracula's Coffin along the way.

BASEMENT OF LOST THINGS

Sleepwalking Tour of Nightmare House

Here is your chance to learn where your weird, creepy dreams get started. Whether you are afraid of giant bugs, closet monsters, or dark basements, this tour includes them all. Nightmare Ned is the perfect guide; he will make sure you don't get lost in someone else's bad dream. So, ten minutes after you fall asleep, Nightmare Ned will meet you in the Deepest, Darkest Place under the porch. Ned lost his extra flashlight on the last tour. See if you can find it before the next nightmare appears!

DANGER!

✦ **SOME OF THE SCARIEST PARTS OF THE TOUR ARE THINGS YOU CAN'T SEE:**
Creaks, groans, and growls!

✦ **BASEMENT OF LOST THINGS**
Ever wonder where all those lost toys end up? This is the place, but beware—it isn't *all* fun and games!

✦ **MOANING MONSTER CLOSET**
Who knows what's inside? No one has ever dared to open the door!

Sleepwalking Tour of Nightmare House

DIRECTIONS

✦ Crawl out from the Deepest, Darkest Place (H6) and sleepwalk west 10 phantom footsteps. Tiptoe up the stairs (F6) to the front door.

✦ Enter Nightmare House and stumble west 5 phantom footsteps into the Library of Lost Books (E5). Continue west into the Dining Room (C5). (Avoid the cracks in the floor, or you might end up in the Basement of Lost Things!)

✦ Walk into the kitchen through the arched door. Find the back stairs and go up to the Hallway of Spooky Shadows (D4–I4). Do not enter the Big Bug Bedroom: the frosty floor is enchanted!

✦ Walk east past Little Bug Bedroom. Pull the cord on the wall to open the door to the secret stairs (F3). Go up for an evil-eye view of the neighborhood (F2). Come back downstairs and continue east down the hall.

✦ Sneak past the Moaning Monster Closet (H4) to the Never-Ending Stairs. Go up into the Terror Turret (I1–I4).

✦ Take the stairs all the way back down to Poltergeist Parlor (G5–I5), where Ned will wake you up and take you home.

Did you find Ned's extra flashlight?

	A	B	C

KEY

5 PHANTOM FOOTSTEPS

Secret Stairs

Forgotten Door

Creaky Step

BIG BUG BEDROOM

DINING ROOM

BASEMENT OF LOST THINGS

SPECIAL POTIONS EXHIBIT

MUSEUM OF HAUNTED OBJECTS

The Museum of Haunted Objects, known as MoHO, is the last stop on our journey. Dr. Jekyll, or perhaps Mr. Hyde, will lead the tour. If you scare easily, pick up an amulet in the Museum Shop of Horrors before the tour begins. Meet in the Rotunda of Possessed Sculpture at the statue of the Headless Horseman. There will be time to browse the rare books of spells and hexes in the museum library. Don't miss the Hall of Die-o-Ramas to view depictions of the most important enchantments of all time. Dr. Jekyll has misplaced a vial of his secret potion. If you find it, please return it to one of the security guards.

DANGER!

✦ ROTUNDA OF POSSESSED SCULPTURE
Beware! Every hour on the hour, the sculptures come alive. For your safety, please do not touch!

✦ HALL OF MYTHICAL OBJECTS
Four Stars! The Lion Cloak of Hercules, Thor's Hammer, the Wicked Witch's Cauldron, and King Arthur's sword, Excalibur!

MUSEUM OF HAUNTED OBJECTS

DIRECTIONS

- Go up the main steps and enter the Rotunda of Possessed Sculpture (I5). Dr. Jekyll will meet you at the statue of the Headless Horseman.

- Exit the rotunda by following Dr. Jekyll through the skull-shaped door (I4), then cross the Floating Bridge until you reach the Spiral Staircase (F4).

- Take the Spiral Staircase all the way down to the first floor, where you can walk the Hall of Mythical Objects (E6). Walk west along the hall 30 zombie steps to the levitator.

- Take the levitator up to the third floor (A4). Need to look up a good spell or a hex? The Spells Library is the place!

- Leave the library by the east door (D3) and enter Checkerboard Hall. Step carefully—some of the squares are trapdoors!

- If you make it safely across Checkerboard Hall, you may enter the Portrait Gallery (E3).

- After viewing the portraits, exit the gallery through the door of Crossed Bones (F2) and carefully cross the Catwalk to the Special Potions Exhibit (H2). (You can look, but don't touch!)

- From the Potions Exhibit, take the Crooked Stairs down one flight to the Ghostly Gallery (H3–J3) for a lovely overview of the Rotunda of Possessed Sculpture.

- After enjoying the view, cross the Floating Bridge again. This time, take the Spiral Staircase down just one level, to the Hall of Die-o-Ramas (F5–A5), a hair-raising display of chilling scenes.

- Walk—don't run—to the museum exit, 37 zombie steps west!

Did you find Dr. Jekyll's missing vial of potion?

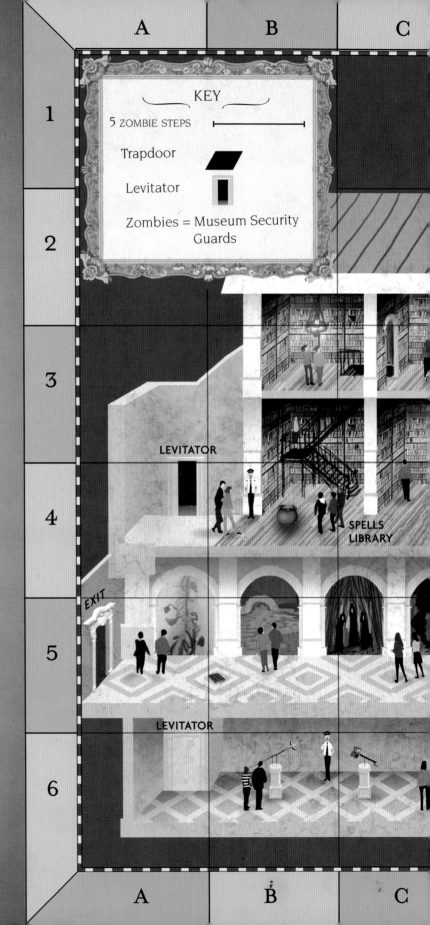

More Thrills and Chills!

Ready to start your journey all over again? Go back, if you dare,
and see what spooky details you might have missed the first time!

THE GHOSTLY GALLEON CRUISE OF THE SEVEN SEAS

- ✦ Captain Davy Jones has all the pirate treasure he needs, but he is hoping to find the lost island of Atlantis. No one has found it yet. Can you?

- ✦ There are 14 sea creatures dwelling in the briny deep. Can you find them all?

LAND of MYTHICAL MONSTERS

- ✦ Athena, the Goddess of Wisdom, has hidden four of her owls. Can you find them?

ROUNDUP OF THE WESTERN TERROR-TORIES

- ✦ Gruesome Gus has hidden three bags of gold from his mining days. Even he can't find them. Can you?

- ✦ Legend has it that the ghost of Clementine can still be seen in these parts. Can you see her?

TOUR OF THE WICKED WOODS AND WITCHFIELD VILLAGE

- ✦ There are thirteen black cats hiding in the Wicked Woods. Can you find them all?

Trip Through Transylvania

✦ There are five banshees hidden along the way. Can you find them . . . before they find you?

Sleepwalking Tour of Nightmare House

✦ See if you can find the three emergency security blankets that Nightmare Ned has put in Nightmare House, just in case you need them.

Museum of Haunted Objects

✦ One of the resident ghosts has taken several books from the library and hidden them in the museum. See if you can find all six.

Help! I'm Lost!

Hidden in each of the seven maps is one object that belongs to another map. See if you can find them.

flashlight
in
MAP 1

spyglass
in
MAP 2

Pegasus
in
MAP 3

bloodmobile
in
MAP 4

dynamite
in
MAP 5

ruby slippers
in
MAP 6

cauldron
in
MAP 7

For hidden object answer key, go to www.candlewick.com/scaryplaces

For Scurvy Boy Brett and
his Pirate Brothers, Mark and Matt
B. G. H.

For my mom and dad,
Felicitas and Silvano Madrid
E. M.

Text copyright © 2012 by B. G. Hennessy
Illustrations copyright © 2012 by Erwin Madrid

First edition 2012

Library of Congress Cataloging-in-Publication Data is available.
Library of Congress Catalog Card Number pending
ISBN 978-0-7636-4541-0

12 13 14 15 16 17 TLF 10 9 8 7 6 5 4 3 2 1

Printed in Dongguan, Guangdong, China

This book was typeset in Novarese.
The illustrations were created digitally.

Candlewick Press
99 Dover Street
Somerville, Massachusetts 02144

visit us at www.candlewick.com